Published in the United States of America by Star Bright Books, Inc.,
30-19 48th Avenue, Long Island City, NY 11101.

The name Star Bright Books and the Star Bright Books logo are registered trademarks of Star Bright Books, Inc. Please visit www.starbrightbooks.com.
For bulk orders, please email: orders@starbrightbooks.com.

Hardback ISBN-13: 978-1-59572-205-8
Paperback ISBN-13: 978-1-59572-206-5

Star Bright Books / NY / 00109100
Printed in China (WKT) 10 9 8 7 6 5 4 3 2 1

Library of Congress Cataloging-in-Publication Data

Coates, Paul.
 Tim and the iceberg / by Paul Coates ; art by Ian P. Benfold Haywood.
     p. cm.
 Summary: On a sweltering day at the beach, Tim sails off in search of an iceberg to cool his grandfather's lemonade.
  ISBN 978-1-59572-205-8 (hardback : alk. paper) -- ISBN 978-1-59572-206-5
 [1. Icebergs--Fiction. 2. Sailing--Fiction. 3. Grandfathers--Fiction.] I. Benfold Haywood, Ian P., ill. II. Title.
 PZ7.C62937Ti 2011
 [E]--dc22
                        2009040880

Tim
and the
Iceberg

By Paul Coates
Illustrated by Ian P. Benfold Haywood

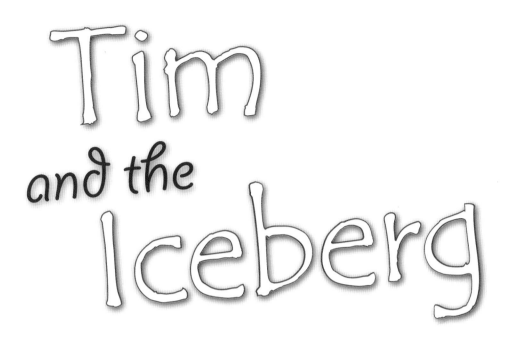

Star Bright Books
New York

One day, Tim and his grandpa were at the beach. Tim was making castles of sand. "Gosh, it's hot," he sighed.

"It sure is," Grandpa agreed.

"Grandpa, have you always lived in hot places?" Tim asked.

"Well," replied Grandpa. "I've lived in lots of places—some even hotter than this, hot enough to make an alligator's tail curl up. And I've been to places so cold that the words froze as I spoke, making icicles grow in my beard. All you could see, for miles and miles, were huge icebergs bigger than houses."

"What's an iceberg?" asked Tim.

"Icebergs are huge mountains of frozen water. Up at the North Pole it's so cold that the land is made of ice. Gigantic chunks break off, crash into the sea, and float. Those are icebergs, Tim."

"We certainly could use one of those right now, it's so hot!" said Tim.

"You're right," agreed Grandpa. "And we could use a drink of lemonade, too."

As he played, Tim had a great idea. "I'll go get an iceberg . . . that will surprise Grandpa . . ."

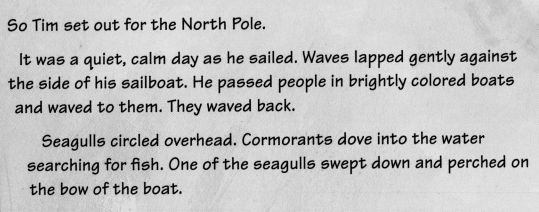

So Tim set out for the North Pole.

It was a quiet, calm day as he sailed. Waves lapped gently against the side of his sailboat. He passed people in brightly colored boats and waved to them. They waved back.

Seagulls circled overhead. Cormorants dove into the water searching for fish. One of the seagulls swept down and perched on the bow of the boat.

Tim travelled north and soon the beach was almost out of sight. Looking ahead, Tim was surprised to see a strange object looming out of the sea.

"I wonder what that is?" Tim thought. "It looks like a skyscraper, but it can't be one, not here in the middle of the sea!"

It was an oil rig. Tim steered close to the rig and shouted to the men standing on the platform. "Ahoy, there! Is this the way to the North Pole?" asked Tim.

"You're right on course," a man wearing a hard hat shouted back.

"I'm going to get an iceberg," Tim hollered.

The men on the platform laughed and waved goodbye to him as he sailed by.

Tim settled back in the boat. Before long, its gentle rocking made him sleepy. He rested his head on the side of the boat and dozed for a while.

When he woke, it was much cooler. Tim found a sweater in the boat and put it on. A mist was drifting low on the sea ahead of him, and soon his sailboat was in the middle of it. A pod of giant blue whales swam alongside his little sailboat. Then the mist began to clear and there, right in front of him was...

. . . a great shimmering white cliff of ice! It towered over his little sailboat.

"Wow! An iceberg! It's huge!" Tim exclaimed.

Tim drew up alongside the iceberg. "How am I going to tow this back?" he wondered.

    Tim found some rope and an iron stake lying at the bottom of the boat. He knew exactly what to do. Grandpa had shown him how to make all kinds of knots.

    Tim tied one end of the rope to his boat. Then he climbed out of the sailboat. He hammered the stake firmly into the side of the iceberg and tied the other end of the rope to the iron stake. "That should work!" he exclaimed.

Tim climbed back into the boat and set sail.

"Here we go," he said. "Won't Grandpa be surprised when he sees the size of this iceberg. It's enormous!"

As Tim sailed south, back through the mist, the great blue whales appeared again for a short time. The air began to feel warmer.

Tim sailed on. The sea was calm. For a while, the only sound Tim heard was the faint lapping of the waves and the friendly cries of the seagulls.

"How far is the shore?" he wondered. Then he saw the oil rig again. As he approached it, the men came running out.

"What do you have there?" they called to him.

"I've got an iceberg!" Tim shouted. "I told you I'd get one!" he said proudly. The men cheered and waved their hats.

But Tim noticed that water was dripping down the side of the iceberg. It was melting in the hot sun. The iceberg was definitely getting smaller . . . and smaller . . . and smaller . . .

Tim took his sweater off. He caught sight of the brightly colored boats once again, and he headed for the shore. There, in the distance, he could see Grandpa walking back from the beach shop. But now, turning around, he saw that his iceberg had shrunk even more!

"Hey, Tim," called out Grandpa, holding up two cups.
"How about that lemonade?"

"Grandpa, I've been to the North Pole!" exclaimed Tim. "I found an iceberg. It was enormous! It was huge . . . bigger than a skyscraper! I've never seen anything so big . . . only . . ." he finished sadly, "it melted!" He held out his hands and showed a little white chunk of ice.

"Wow, Tim!" cried Grandpa. "A tiny iceberg! That's terrific. It's just what we need for our lemonade!"

With a laugh, Tim split the ice in two, and dropped a little lump into each cup.

"Delicious!" said Grandpa.

"Yummy!" said Tim.

And they sat on the beach and drank up their nice cool drinks.